A FAMILY LIKE MINE

AGES 4-8

COLORING AND ACTIVITY BOOK

Color By Numbers

1. Orange   2. Yellow   3. Green
4. Blue   5. Red   6. Black

Color By Numbers

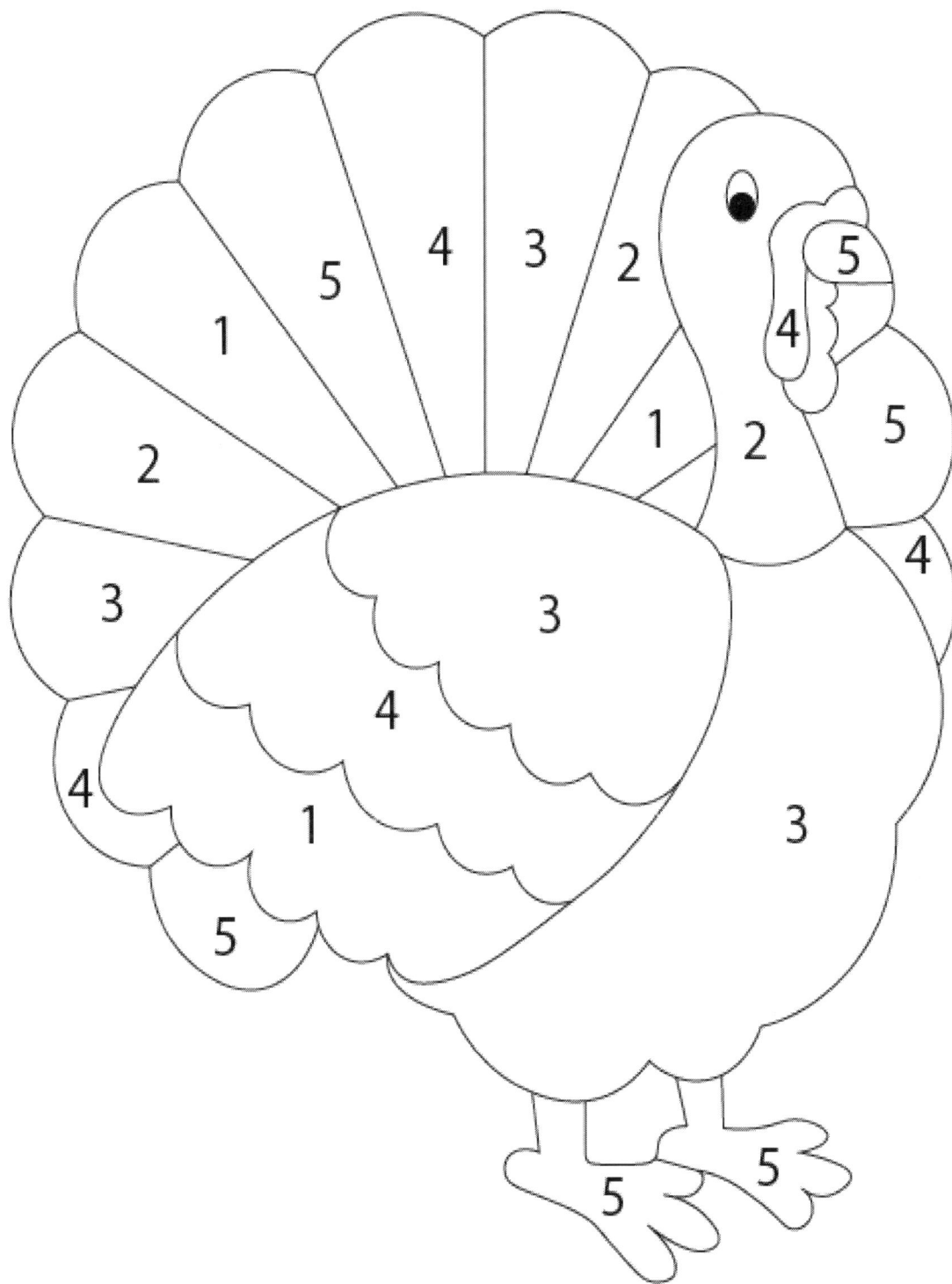

1. Blue   2. Orange   3. Brown

4. Red   5. Yellow

Color By Numbers

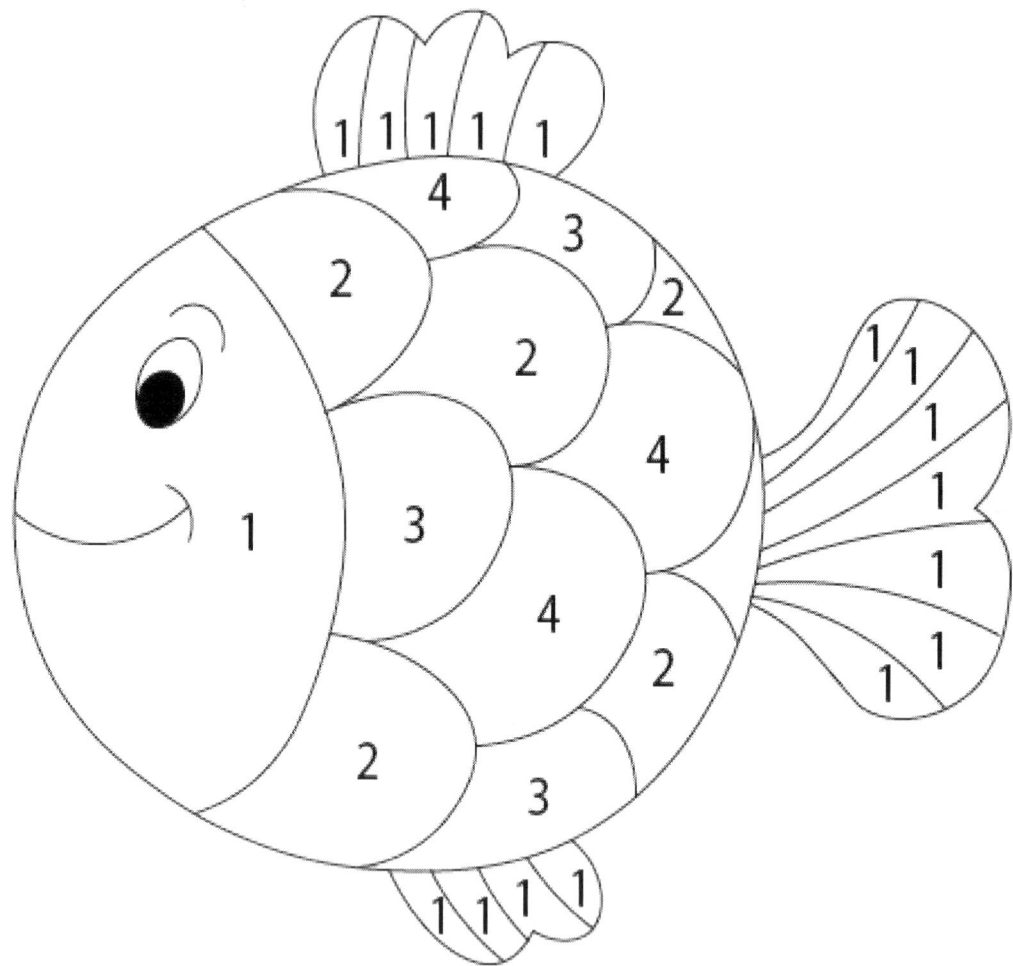

1. Yellow   2. Red   3. Orange   4. Pink

Color By Numbers

1. Rose   2. Skin   3. Light Blue
4. Green   5. Pink   6. Yellow

Tracing

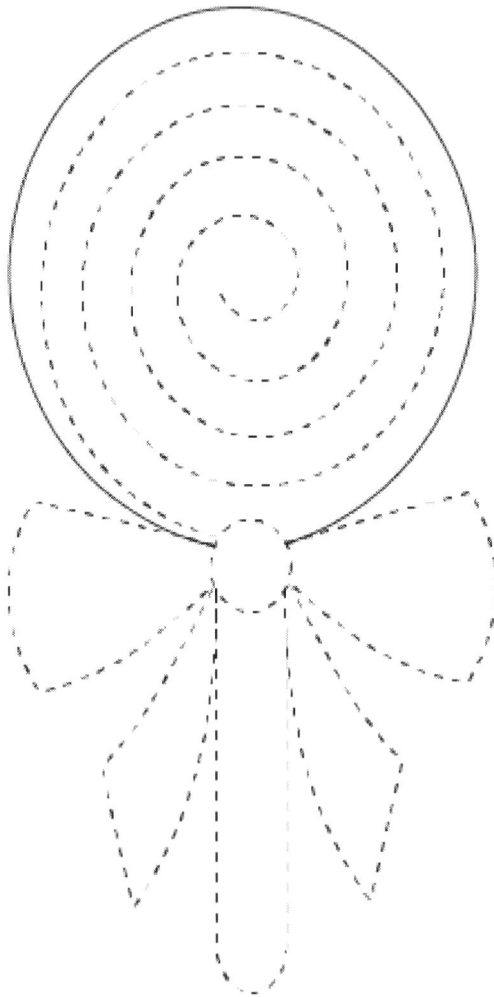

Tracing

Tracing

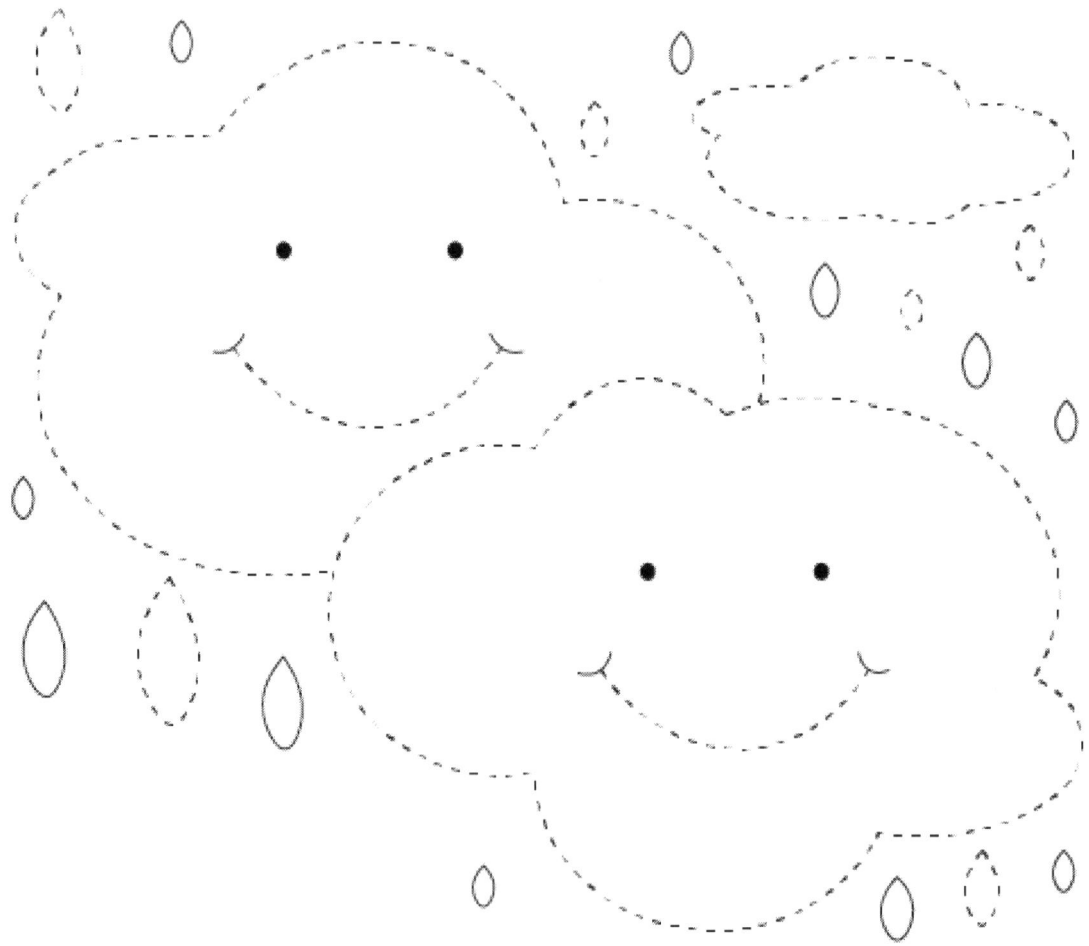

Connect the Dots

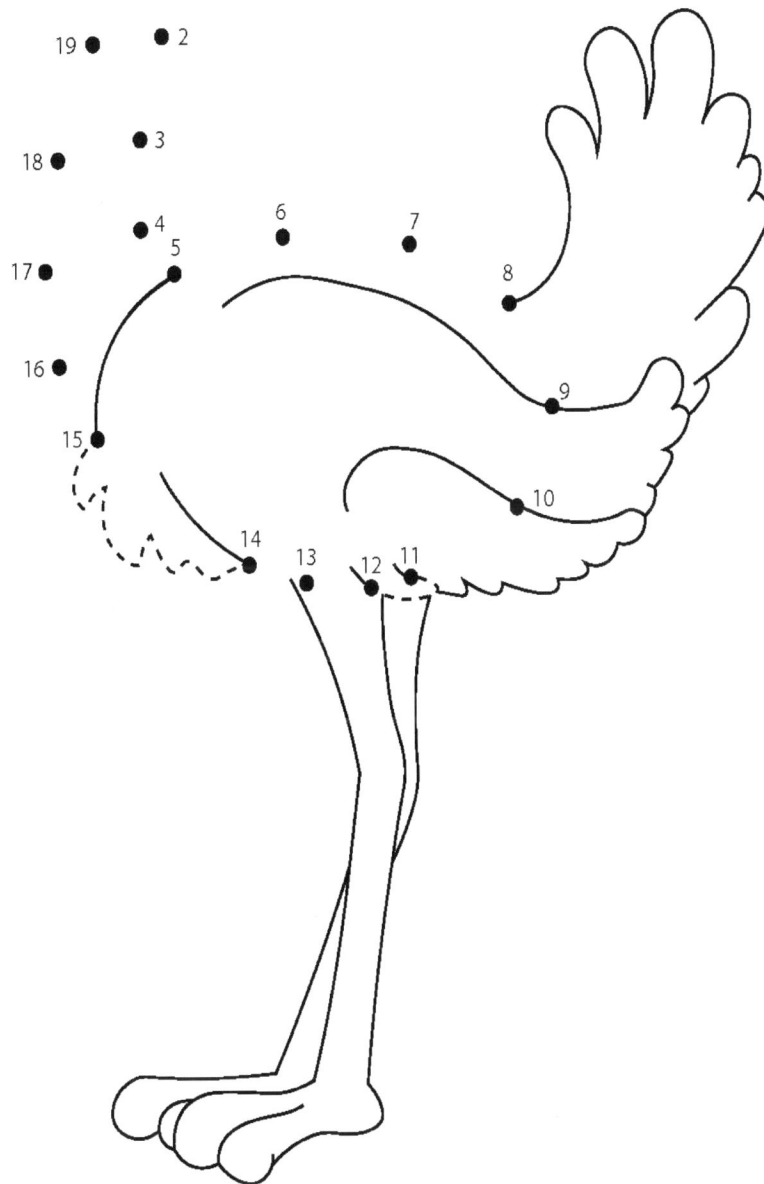

Connect the Dots

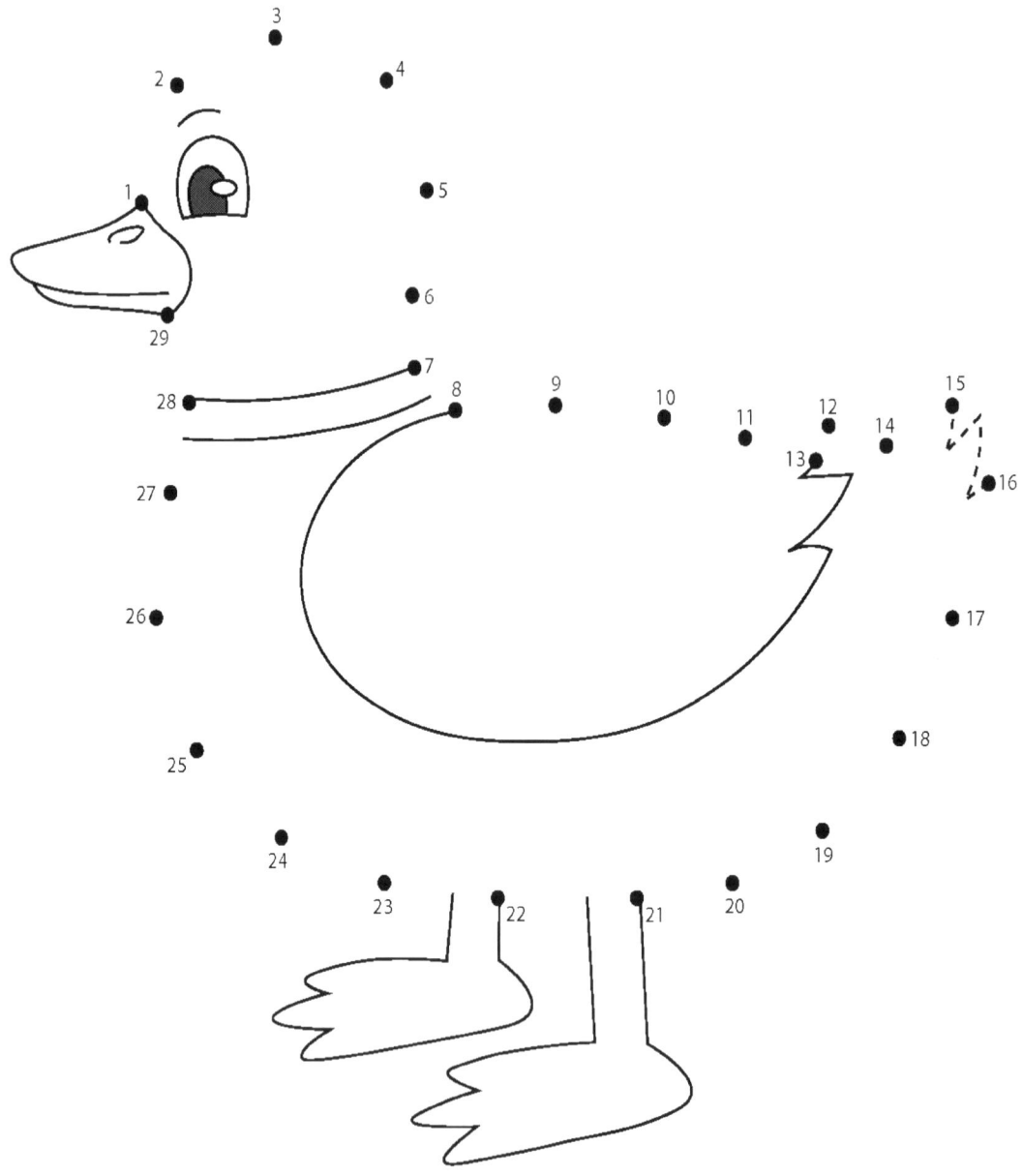

Connect the Dots

Connect the Dots

Rectantle Maze

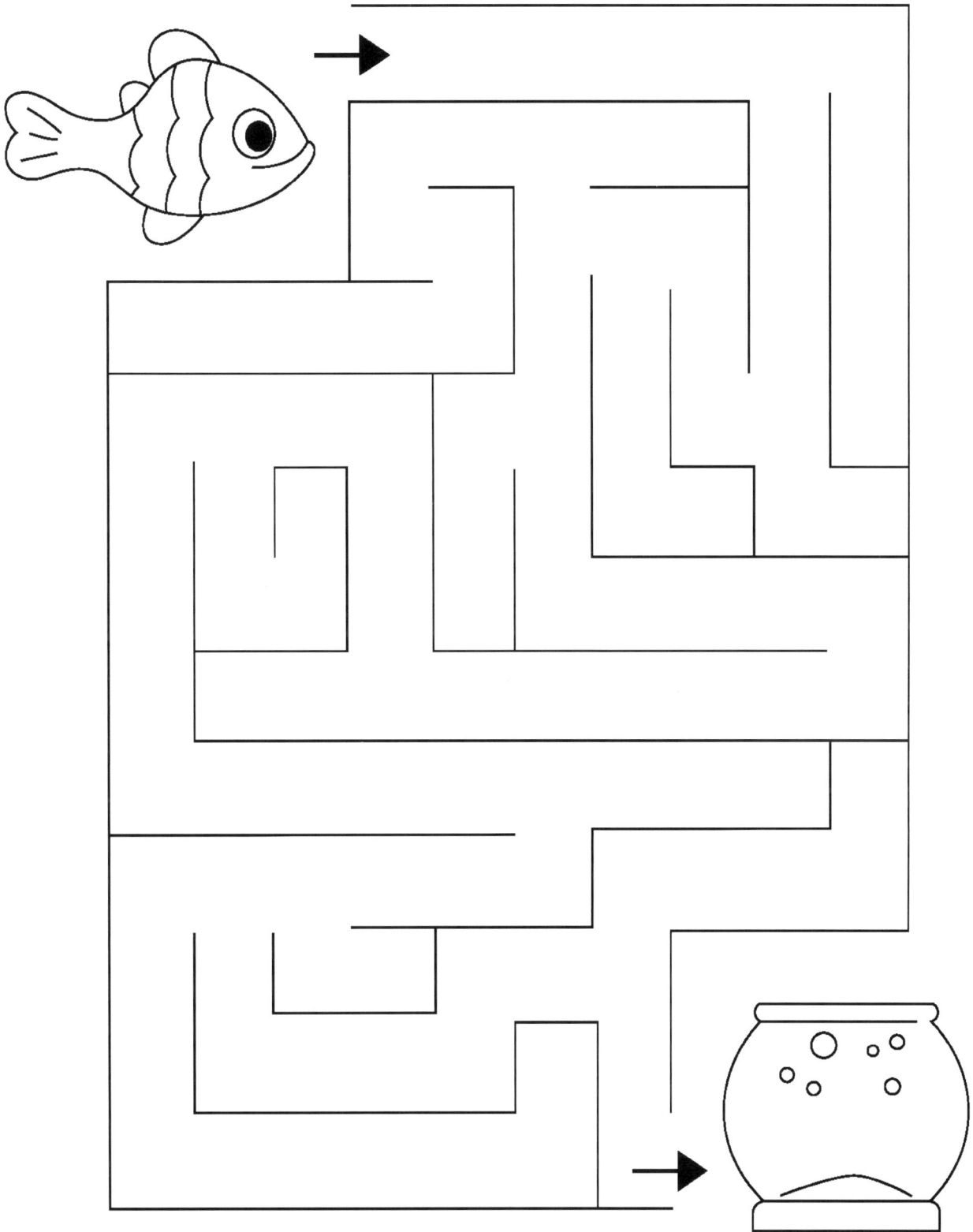

World Search

I	Z	H	D	S	Z	Y	U	O	M	A	D
O	S	T	R	O	H	S	Y	N	D	I	Y
S	R	E	M	A	D	W	R	O	N	D	Z
N	Y	A	E	S	A	I	Y	S	M	Y	A
N	D	H	Y	Z	I	M	Z	E	A	N	R
Y	P	A	I	L	O	Y	S	Y	O	Z	M
T	M	A	D	R	A	N	D	I	A	R	E
P	C	I	S	L	A	S	N	A	Z	D	T
O	R	A	M	A	S	I	C	O	E	C	I
S	A	N	B	D	K	L	O	B	S	Y	K
O	T	S	Z	I	R	R	I	S	P	A	S
Y	E	A	B	T	N	E	N	D	R	Z	O

Bikini	Shorts	Sunny	Cabin
Swim	Kite	Pail	Ice

World Search

O	S	R	M	A	D	R	A	E	S	A	M
A	N	Y	E	S	A	M	P	D	N	Z	O
P	L	Z	F	A	M	I	L	Y	N	Y	A
A	I	O	M	P	A	L	N	D	R	Z	I
D	B	A	E	A	N	O	R	Y	Z	D	O
C	H	O	M	R	L	N	E	A	W	M	O
I	A	N	Y	K	O	L	H	T	S	O	A
N	M	D	N	O	S	M	T	O	F	S	N
C	I	S	N	M	S	R	A	A	N	G	H
I	R	B	O	Z	M	Y	F	P	S	I	A
P	A	Y	M	A	D	R	Z	L	O	R	M
O	T	V	A	C	A	T	I	O	N	L	Y

Family	Picnic	Son	Girl
Father	Vacation	Food	Park

Color By Numbers

1. Yellow   2. Orange   3. Purple

4. Black   5. Green

Color By Numbers

1. Brown   2. Green   3. Yellow

Color By Numbers

1. Yellow   2. Blue   3. Red

4. Green   5. Brown   6. Orange

Square Maze

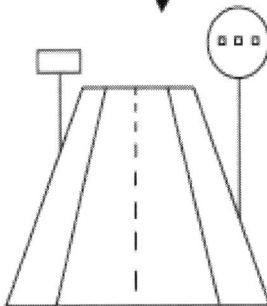

Circle Maze

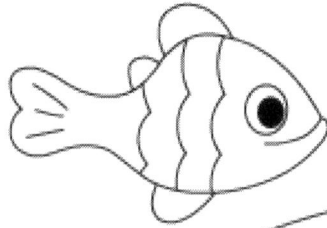

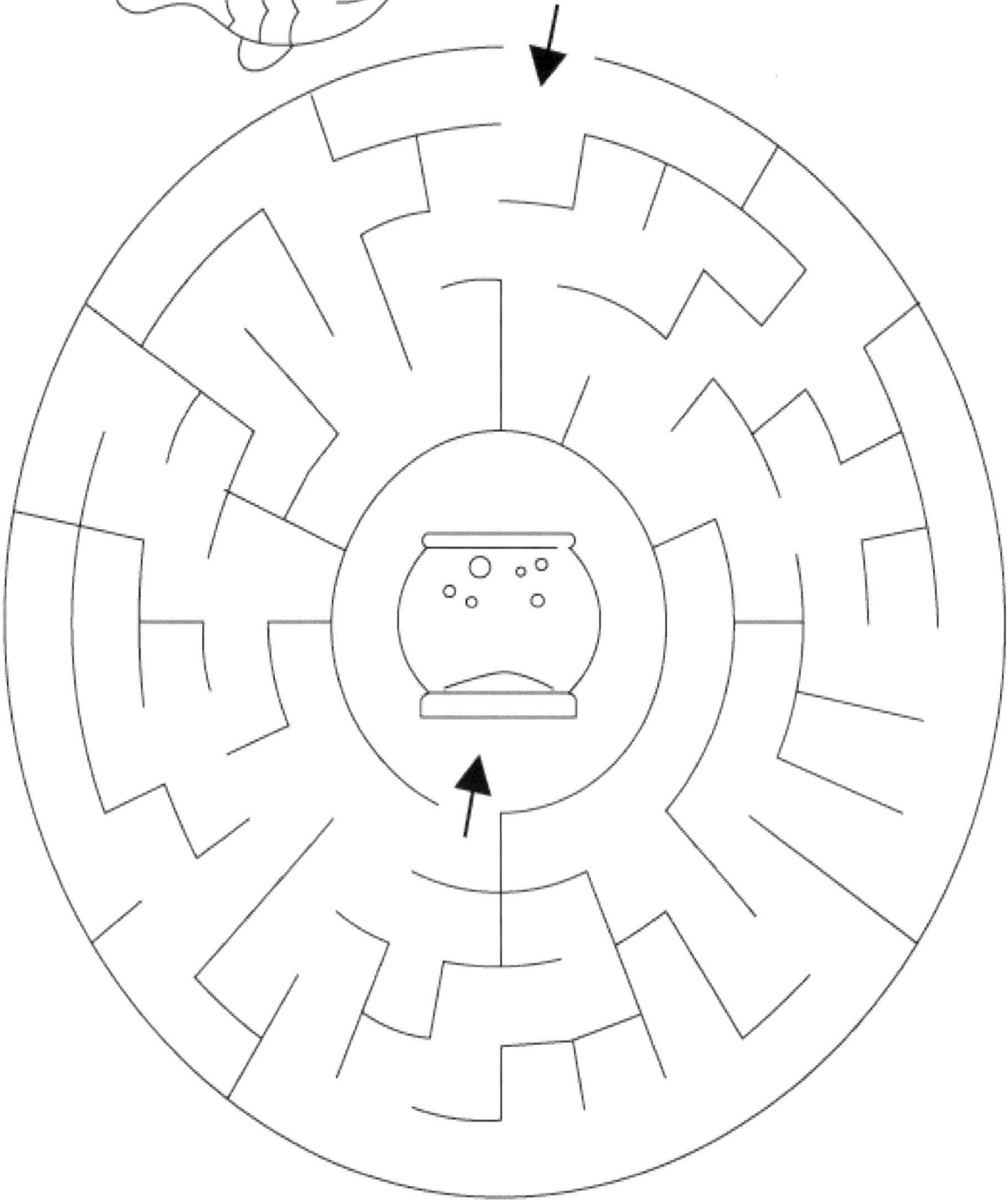

Triangle Maze

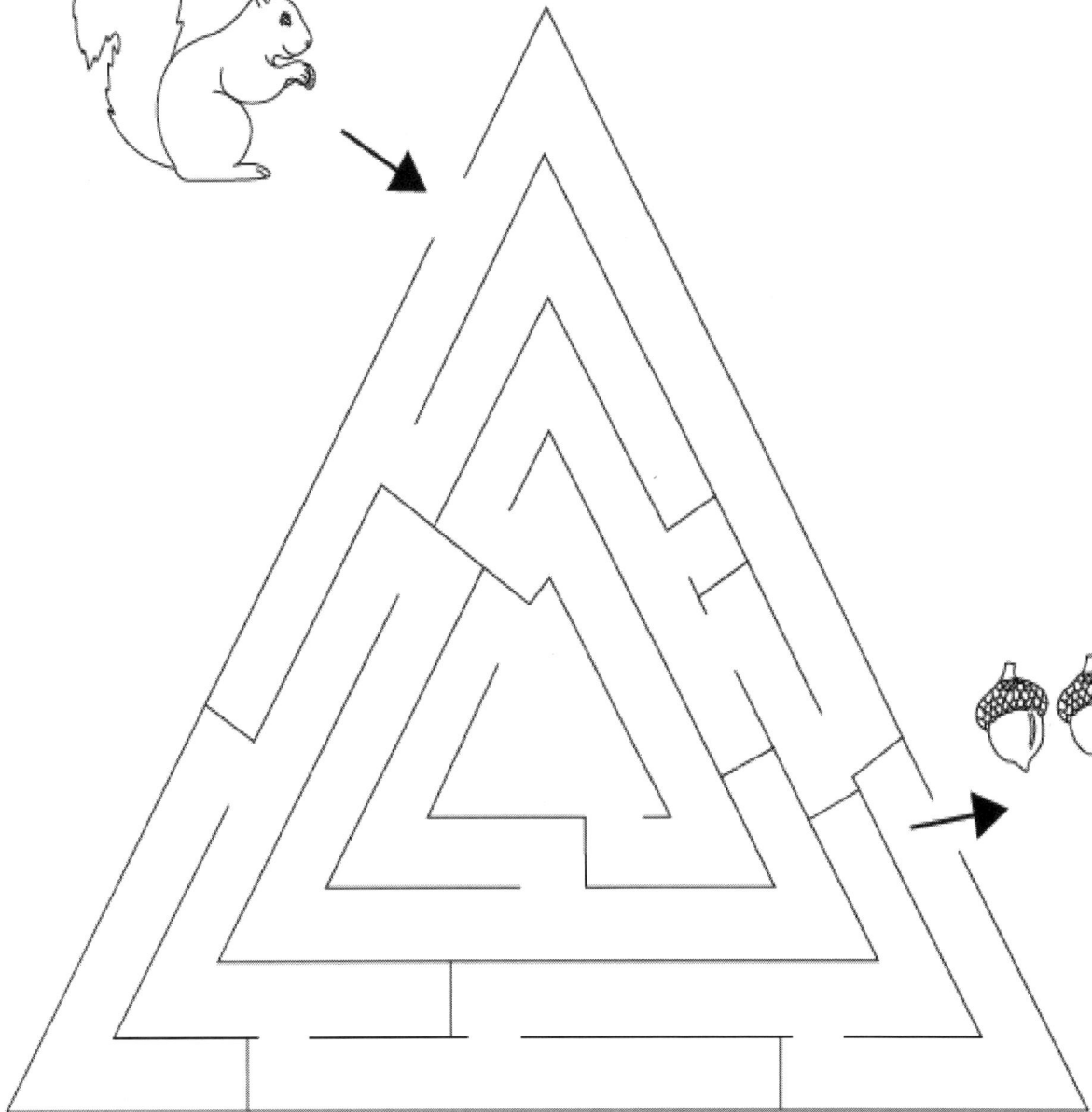

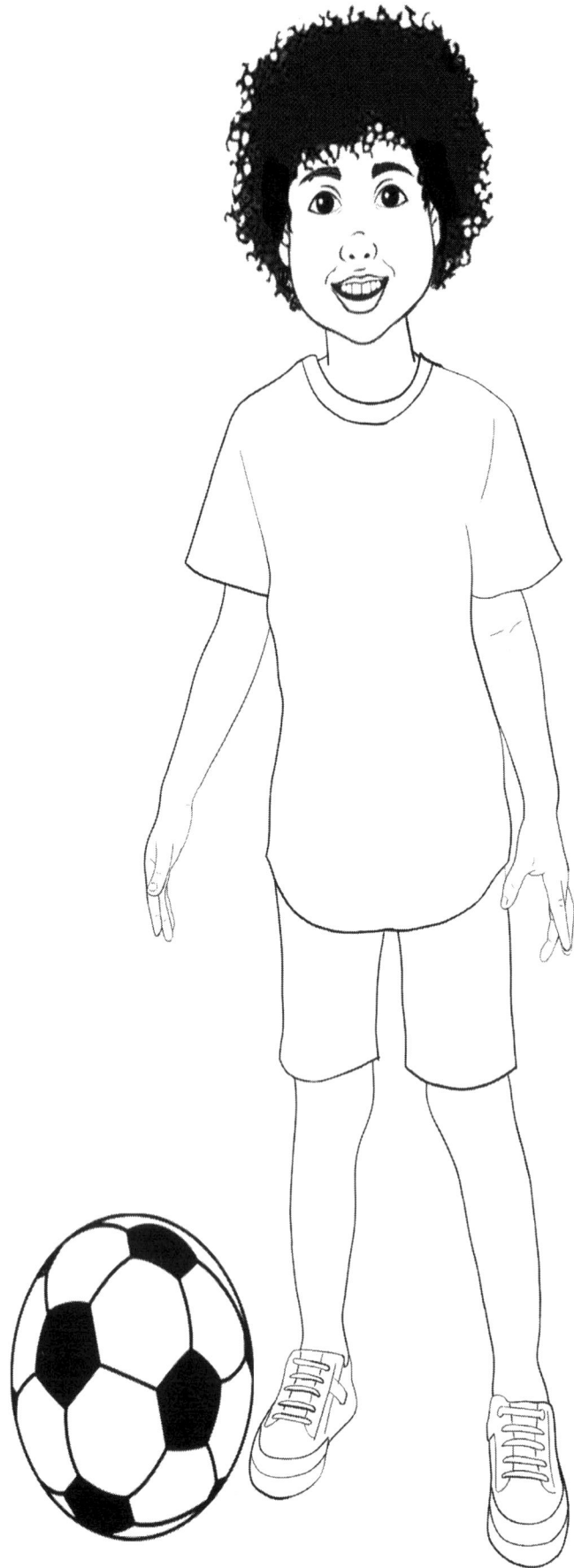

World Search

I	Z	H	D	S	Z	Y	U	O	M	A	D
O	S	T	R	O	H	S	Y	N	D	I	Y
S	R	E	M	A	D	W	R	O	N	D	Z
N	Y	A	E	S	A	Y	S	M	Y	A	
N	D	H	Y	Z	I	M	Z	E	A	N	R
Y	P	A	I	L	O	Y	S	Y	O	Z	M
T	M	A	D	R	A	N	D	I	A	R	E
P	C	I	S	L	A	S	N	A	Z	D	T
O	R	A	M	A	S	I	C	O	E	C	I
S	A	N	B	D	K	L	O	B	S	Y	K
O	T	S	Z	I	R	R	I	S	P	A	S
Y	E	A	B	T	N	E	N	D	R	Z	O

Bikini	Shorts	Sunny	Cabin
Swim	Kite	Pail	Ice

World Search

O	S	R	M	A	D	R	A	E	S	A	M
A	N	Y	E	S	A	M	P	D	N	Z	O
P	L	Z	F	A	M	I	L	Y	N	Y	A
A	I	O	M	P	A	L	N	D	R	Z	I
D	B	A	E	A	N	O	R	Y	Z	D	O
C	H	O	M	R	L	N	E	A	W	M	O
I	A	N	Y	K	O	L	H	T	S	O	A
N	M	D	N	O	S	M	T	O	F	S	N
C	I	S	N	M	S	R	A	A	N	G	H
I	R	B	O	Z	M	Y	F	P	S	I	A
P	A	Y	M	A	D	R	Z	L	O	R	M
O	T	V	A	C	A	T	I	O	N	L	Y

Family	Picnic	Son	Girl
Father	Vacation	Food	Park

Rectantle Maze

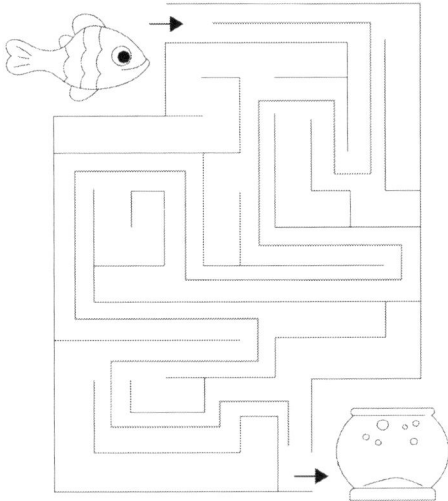

Circle Maze

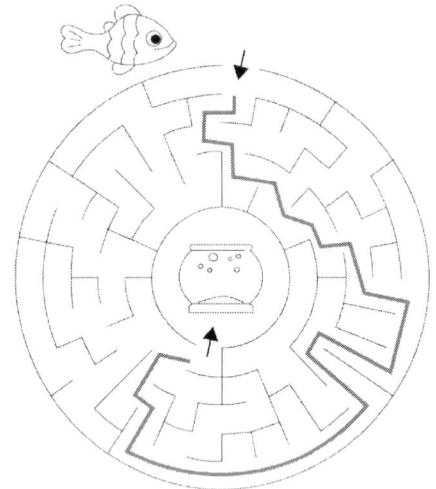

Triangle Maze

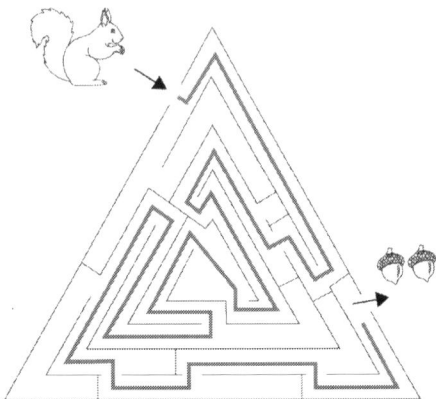

Square Maze

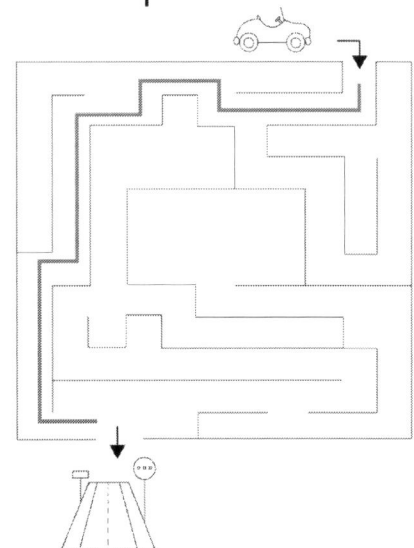

Made in the USA
Las Vegas, NV
09 December 2023